Dear Parents:

Congratulations! Your child is taking the first steps on an exciting journey. The destination? Independent reading!

STEP INTO READING® will help your child get there. The program offers five steps to reading success. Each step includes fun stories and colorful art or photographs. In addition to original fiction and books with favorite characters, there are Step into Reading Non-Fiction Readers, Phonics Readers and Boxed Sets, Sticker Readers, and Comic Readers—a complete literacy program with something to interest every child.

Learning to Read, Step by Step!

Ready to Read Preschool–Kindergarten
• big type and easy words • rhyme and rhythm • picture clues
For children who know the alphabet and are eager to begin reading.

Reading with Help Preschool–Grade 1
• basic vocabulary • short sentences • simple stories
For children who recognize familiar words and sound out new words with help.

Reading on Your Own Grades 1–3
• engaging characters • easy-to-follow plots • popular topics
For children who are ready to read on their own.

Reading Paragraphs Grades 2–3
• challenging vocabulary • short paragraphs • exciting stories
For newly independent readers who read simple sentences with confidence.

Ready for Chapters Grades 2–4
• chapters • longer paragraphs • full-color art
For children who want to take the plunge into chapter books but still like colorful pictures.

STEP INTO READING® is designed to give every child a successful reading experience. The grade levels are only guides; children will progress through the steps at their own speed, developing confidence in their reading.

Remember, a lifetime love of reading starts with a single step!

BARBIE and associated trademarks and trade dress are owned by, and used under license from, Mattel.
Copyright © 2020 Mattel. All Rights Reserved.
www.barbie.com
Published in the United States by Random House Children's Books, a division of Penguin Random House LLC, 1745 Broadway, New York, NY 10019, and in Canada by Penguin Random House Canada Limited, Toronto.

Step into Reading, Random House, and the Random House colophon are registered trademarks of Penguin Random House LLC.

Visit us on the Web!
StepIntoReading.com
rhcbooks.com

Educators and librarians, for a variety of teaching tools, visit us at RHTeachersLibrarians.com

ISBN 978-0-593-12759-9 (trade) — ISBN 978-0-593-12760-5 (lib. bdg.)

Printed in the United States of America
10 9 8 7 6 5 4 3 2 1

The Mermaid Park Mystery

based on the original screenplay by
Arthur Brown & Douglas Sloan

Random House 🏠 New York

Barbie and her friends
are so excited.

They will work together at the Mermaid Water Park.

Nikki loves art.
She will be
a face painter.

Daisy loves
taking pictures.
She will be
a photographer.

Renee wears
a whale costume.
She will pose
for photos.

Teresa will make
and sell
yummy treats.

Ken will take care of
a lost baby whale.
He will feed and care
for her until
her family comes.

Barbie will direct
the water park's big show.
They will perform
a mermaid musical!

Barbie and her friends
work hard.
They also have fun.

They get to try
all the rides!
Whee!

Mr. Pearlman is
the new owner.
He wants Barbie
to run the water park.

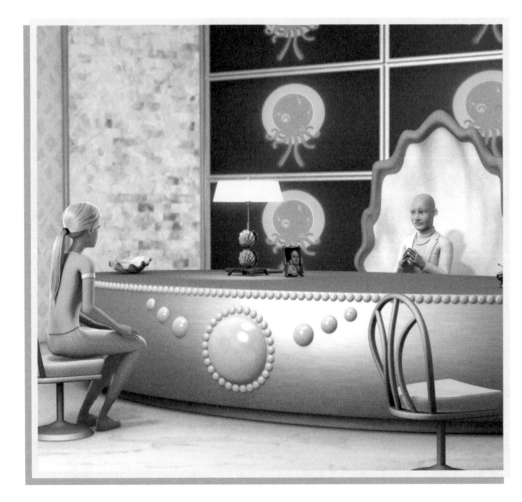

Barbie sees

something strange.

She spots a truck

on the dock.

Scuba divers take

a box out of the water.

Barbie and Ken
wait until dark.
They spot a boat.

Mr. Pearlman owns
the boat.
He sends scuba divers
into the water.

Barbie and Ken
follow the divers.

The divers
are stealing
rare purple pearls!

A diver sets up
an electric fence.
No one else can get to
the purple pearls.
The whale family
cannot get to their baby.

Barbie and Ken
tell their friends
that Mr. Pearlman
is stealing pearls.

Barbie comes up
with a plan.

Barbie sneaks into
Mr. Pearlman's office.
She learns the code
to the electric fence.

Barbie's friends turn off
the electric fence.
The whale family
can be with their baby.

Mr. Pearlman and
his divers try to escape.

Barbie and Ken
fly in a helicopter.
They chase
Mr. Pearlman's boat.

The whale family
helps, too.
They bump and
stop the boat.

Barbie and Ken
catch Mr. Pearlman.

They give each
other a high five
for a job well done.

Later,
Barbie and her friends
celebrate.

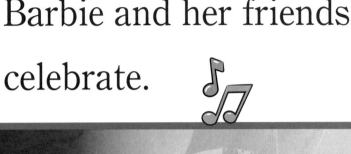

They sing and dance
in the mermaid
musical.

Barbie and her friends
have had an
amazing adventure!